When Prayers Change Things
Written by: Christopher C. Smith

2

Christopher C. Smith
Father, Author, Actor, Independent Publisher & Song Writer

Thank you's & Dedications

First I would like to give thanks to God

My Beautiful Mother
Ora Henderson

My Beautiful Daughter
Lauren Madison Smith

My Supportive A.O.D Family

My Beautiful sister Valerie Hayes, My niece Valyn My nephews Vashon and D.J.,Cash Blocka My Canada family, Darrell Washington ,Bugs Money & Jocelyn, Yeti, Ryan Levin & 4sure ent. Shacora Johnson, My Entire Philly Family, My whole Yonkers & Bronx Family, Moe Dirdee, Nikki & Amy, My whole Detroit Family Rory, Rigo, Robert Jackson & Every Body at the Wal-Mart #5404 Store, DJ Antonio and the wonderful Staff at Wal-Mart Radio !!!

Sponsored By

Contact by Email
Contact@famlyinc.com

Sponsored By

Ryan Levin & 4 Sure Ent.

Contact Info: Ryan@4suredjs.com

Sponsored By

Wal-Mart Radio
Antonio Williams & Bo Woloszyn

Contact Info: 855-925-7346

THE PRELUDE

"SOLD!" The dealer shouted with enthusiasm, slightly winking his right eye.

It seemed strange but I was overwhelmed with excitement myself so I brushed it off.

I reached over to shake his hand.

"I really can't believe this," I said happily. I was so anxious closing out the deal my palms began to sweat. A few moments passed and all was complete. I smiled to myself almost shedding a tear as a warm and amazing feeling came over me.

All of my hard work had finally paid off.

After spending three years being homeless and working my butt off,

I was finally a proud owner of a new 2017 Cadillac Escalade.

For once, it seemed like everything I prayed for was coming to existence.

As the dealer handed over the keys, I couldn't count the number of times I thanked him.

"Oh! No problem, Mr. Martinez! It is with great pleasure and nice doing business with you.

"Here! Take a card," he offered.

I thanked him once more before I quickly hurried off to my new car. I was so happy I did not know who I should tell the good news first. So I didn't call anyone. I hopped in the wheel, started it up and drove off the lot with the biggest smile a man could bear.

It was a short ride before I noticed a detour sign on the main road. The police were doing a random license and insurance check. I slowly pulled up to the nearest officer who signaled for me to roll down my window.

"License and insurance, please," he asked with a firm tone in his voice.

I parked the car then reached into my pocket to hand him what he asked for.

I rolled the window up then sat back patiently, waiting for him to return to my car and allow me to proceed home. Unfortunately, it took longer than expected but that didn't dull the excitement of my most recent purchase.

I busied myself by going through my phone trying to decide who I should inform of my latest acquisition. I had finally started to call my wife when I heard a loud knock on my window.

With a slightly startled look on my face I rolled the window down again.

Before I could say anything the officer started asking me awkward and demanding questions about my car.

Like when it was purchased and where. I graciously answered him with as much detail as possible and also passed him my paper work. The officer took the papers, glancing over them briefly then insisted I stepped out of the car.

"I need to do a quick search, Mr. Martinez," he said.

"Do you have anything illegal or hazardous in this car before I start the search?" he questioned.

With an even stranger look on my face I replied. "No. I just bought the car, sir. I don't have anything in it." I watched in silence as the officer rummaged through the SUV, flashing his light around here and there.

I sat on the side of the road for a while, observing the search as other cars went by slower than necessary. The drivers were more than likely too busy observing me but I did not let that bother me. It was not until multiple squad cars pulled up, surrounding my car when I started to worry. As I gazed from my position on the curb I noticed one cop direct another to see what looked like a small brown bag tucked under the driver's seat.

From my distance I yelled to the officers. "Is everything okay?"

Slowly I stood up and walked toward my car to see what was going on.

"Stand back! Put your hands up, over your head!"

I heard a few officers shout loudly and aggressively. "Get on the ground, now!"

I knelt down and followed their instructions as I started to feel scared and more nervous than I had ever been in my life.

"What's wrong?" I said with my face to the ground and my hands in the air. A short, stocky officer patted me down while the first officer grilled me.

This time he was even more firm, forward and aggressive when he spoke.

"I'm going to ask you again, sir, and don't play dumb with me. Do you have any illegal stuff on you?"

"No, sir! No! I don't have anything, I just bought this car!" Absolute confusion covered my face. I repeated my story about just buying the car and being clueless of his allegations. "What are you talking about? What did I do wrong? I have no idea what's going on."

"Don't play dumb," the officer yelled. "So you thought I wasn't gone find out, huh?"

"No, Sir! What are you talking about?"

With slight force he lowered my upraised arms and started reading me my rights. Before you know it I was put in hand cuffs and motioned to the back of the police car.

I couldn't help but put my head down in confusion, attempting to think of what it was that I could have possibly did wrong.

As I silently started to pray I felt the car move and before you know it I was walking into the police station.

With a blank stare on my face still mixed up about what was going on, I started to demand answers.

"Excuse me? What the hell is going on," I said with a very angry tone. That was when one of the officers finally told me what it was I was being accused for.

I stood there in disbelief. I was being charged with carrying drugs, used needles and a small switchblade that contained blood on it. All things that I had nothing to do with—I didn't even know they were stashed in the car.

"Get your rest," a detective said while walking pass, "you will see the judge first thing tomorrow morning to determine what's going to happen.

Here in Smithville we take drugs and murder cases very seriously."

"Murder?" I said with extreme shock, "But I didn't kill anybody!" I fell to the floor crying then asked if at the very least I could use a nearby phone to notify my wife of my whereabouts.

"Sorry, it's late. Everyone has gone home and where we keep the phone for you to make your call, the door is locked. I don't have the key."

The detective's name was Lauren.

She guided me to my holding cell.
Where I prayed until I fell asleep.

Chapter 1

I sat in my cell for what seemed like forever after making all the necessary calls. How was it that my entire life was turned upside down in just a matter of minutes?

"Hurry up!" An officer yelled from the other side of the bars. "Pack your stuff!

Time to see the judge."

I quickly gathered my belongings to get as prepared as I possibly could.

While walking through the door of the court room I couldn't help but notice everyone was there for me as my eyes got watery and tears began to slowly roll down my cheeks.

"We love you, Erick!" My wife softly shouted across the room to me. I slowly turned around to wave at everyone but as happy as I was to see them I was still hurt about the situation in general. I was still in such disbelief and almost regretted how one of the proudest moments and decisions of my life, also ruined it in a matter of minutes. I lowered my head down to further think and sulk but I felt a slight touch on my shoulder.

"Hi! My name is Michael Norman. I will be representing you throughout this case."

"Oh? Thank you, so much!" I said as I eagerly rose up from my seat to hug him gratefully. "For a second, I thought I was going to be alone."

"No sir!

When your wife contacted me about your situation I knew for a fact that this was going to be an easy victory."

As we went over what happened that day I learned exactly what the consequences were and time I was facing. To my surprise the crimes were classified as second degree felonies with sentences totaling 3-9 years. Amidst hearing that I instantly felt my stomach turn inside out and my legs started to go numb.

"But don't worry," Michael assured, "everything is under control and justice will be served. Now, just sit tight and the judge will be here shortly."

A few moments passed then the bailiff entered the room. From there I knew it was about to go down. Silently, I said a quick prayer.

"All rise," the bailiff bellowed. "The Court of the Smithville Judicial Circuit, criminal division, is now in session. The Honorable Judge Nelson Smith is presiding."

I took a deep breath as the sweat formed across my forehead. I was worried. With the way things had been going, who knew what the outcome of this mess would be.

"Everyone but the jury may be seated.

Mr. Smith, please swear in the jury," Judge Ortiz said with a smooth tone carrying over the courtroom motioning the bailiff.

"Hello, your honor," my lawyer, Michael spoke after the formalities were finished. "How are you today?" He and the judge made eye contacts and Judge Ortiz nodded to him as if permitting him to continue.

"My client, Erick Martinez, purchased a car not too long ago as to which he did not know that it had the items that we have before us and is being used against us as evidence. Take a note that these items were stashed in the car."

"Well sir, where is your witness?" The judge questioned. Not noticing any movement from our defense he continued. "How do we know that your client, Mr. Martinez, had nothing to do with the crimes he has been accused of?"

"Well, your honor," Michael said, "I, myself, have contacted the dealer and he said he will be here shortly."

The judge then looked my way and asked my lawyer if I would like to take the stand to explain my side of the story. With a clump of coal lodged in my throat and anxiety showing all over my face I did my best to whisper to Michael that I was not ready at the moment. I was still kind of in shock and needed time to get my thoughts and words together.

"But Erick," my lawyer said with a troubled tone, "this is your time to get ahead and put out your story, which is the truth. It is the least you can do and even still, they'd really have to try their hardest to hammer us."

"Okay," I agreed.

"Excuse me, your honor. My client, Erick Martinez, will take the stand and explain everything."

"Okay," the judge said, "come up to the stand."

I got up slowly and proceeded to the bench. I was greeted by the bailiff with a bible to swear upon while raising my right hand. I was then asked by my lawyer to inform the courtroom of the events that took place on the day in question. I explained my entire day from when I woke up to the time I was pulled over and arrested.

"Well Erick, I have one quick question," the judge said with a very serious look and stern voice, "as you bought this car from the dealer you did not check the car at all?"

"Well ss-sir," I said with a slight stutter. "No, I honestly didn't. If anything, I was more excited that I was able to have purchased my first car. And was even more excited to drive and surprise my wife who was at the time was at home waiting on me."

As I continued to tell my story and answer the questions the judge asked me I noticed the dealer making his way through the doors finding a seat behind my lawyer.

"But your honor, had I known that this car had such items inside I would have never bought the car. I probably would have called the police myself."

I wrapped up my story and was permitted to return to my seat. My lawyer let it be known that the dealer had arrived and that he would be the next witness to take the stand.

"That's fine," Judge Ortiz agreed, "but first I will like to issue a continuation and this trial will continue two weeks from today. Court is adjourned!" He slammed his wooden gavel.

I was so nervous I didn't know I had began to stare in space and the sound of the gavel slamming had brought me back to life.

"It's going to be okay," my wife said as she made her way over to me and proceeded to give me the tightest hug ever. "Everything will be okay."

She couldn't help but break down in tears as I held her hands in mine and regretted not being able to go home and console her through this pain. She was feeling everything I was feeling and it was hard seeing her this way. I know she felt the same way about me.

We all made our way to the hallway I couldn't help but notice the dealer redirect his gaze as we neared. He was acting shifty, as if he was avoiding interactions with me purposely—as if he had something else up his sleeve. I felt in my heart that he was going to put the blame all on me. But why?

I fell fast asleep the first night returning to my cell but the weight of trial and circumstances fell deeply into place the next day. I became so stressed. I barely slept and ate irregularly. And time definitely was not on my side.

Before I knew it, my next court date was finally upon me.

A single random officer chaperoned me the entire journey from my cell to the court room. I couldn't help but notice the dealer sitting alone a few pews behind the defense's bench amongst entering. As the officer allowed me to sit I felt a since of urgency overcome me. Before I realized or could think more about my actions I was talking.

"So, what's up?" I asked as I turned around and motioned to shake his hand. I could tell he was anxious. Almost as if he expected animosity from me. All I wanted was answers.

"Nothing much," he said as his voice began to crack and lose its deep vibrant tone that he had the last time we spoke.

"So what happened? Why was all that stuff in the car? Was this some type of set up, man?" I felt myself getting frustrated as I briefly explained how crazy my life was since I left his lot.

"Well, I apologize sir but I have no idea what was going on," the dealer spoke as he turned his head, searching for any escape out of the conversation possible. His face was plain, a poker face and his voice didn't really show any concern for my misfortune. I wanted to say more. But I knew wasn't going to get more.

Just then the doors of the court room opened and my wife and lawyer walked through. I stood up to greet them, annoyed and angry at my conversation with the dealer.

"How are you holding up?" My lawyer Michael questioned as my wife planted a warm smooth kiss on the side of my forehead.

"Good morning, honey," her voice was soft as a lullaby I missed her so much.

Reading my body language she looked deep into my eyes and assured,
"Everything will be okay."

"Well, Erick,"

Michael interrupted, his hands moved shiftily breaking our gaze as if he was jealous of our moment.

"I'm going to try to do the best I can to beat this guy but I'll be honest, all of a sudden he has amnesia and claims he doesn't know what's going on which makes the outcome of everything unknown.

If anything, I can ask for another continuation and we can try to work out a plea deal to at least get the charges reduced to a misdemeanor or possibly having this whole case thrown out because to me this is complete nonsense from the jump."

"No," I said allowing my anger to show while not causing a large scene, "*trying*, is not a solution to this problem, Michael. I need you to beat this coward!

I can't afford to lose this case and go to jail another day, man. Did you hear them?
They are talking about giving me 3 years minimum—for something I did NOT do—when I have a wife at home!" I shook my head and returned to my seat.

Tears almost welled up in my eyes, I was so emotional and knew this was not the proper forum to lash out the way I needed to. It was just so frustrating not being able to *be* yourself.

Your every moved watched. Your future and freedom, literally in someone else's hands. Again, I silently asked God—*Why*?

My wife ran her hands over my shoulders and handed me a Kleenex before she went to seat herself in the first pew.

Michael just sat down in silence, shifting through papers for the few moments we waited for the trial to begin.

"All rise!" The bailiff directed once the judge arrived. They carried out the formalities and we picked up where we left off two weeks prior.

"Mr. Norman, you may proceed with your witness,"

the judge motioned. I looked at Michael.

I could tell his nerves had returned. He stood awkwardly and abruptly, calling the dealer to come and speak.

There was something about the way the dealer walked.

Maybe I was just in my head but everything about him seemed arrogant, conniving and misleading.

As he stood at the stand, placed his handle on the bible and agreed to his oath,

I could not ignore the resent and anger I then felt, witnessing him lie and deny his involvement to anything going on with that car with a straight face.

Deep down inside I was a raging inferno. This court case was going downhill fast. I felt my life shattering.

So I looked back and blew a kiss to my wife and all of the others that came in effort to support me because due to this con artist, I knew for a fact that more jail time would soon follow.

Chapter 2

I was actually confused as the judge slammed his gavel and called for one last continuation in order for the dealer to get his things together. In fact, I have never felt so puzzled in my life. All the dealer had to do from the start was tell the truth. It seemed to me that only lies need to be prepared. But that was only me.

"Court will continue tomorrow at the same time," Judge Ortiz had commanded.

My head dropped deep into my chest and my shoulders sank.

At that very moment I knew it would be best to prepare myself for the hard time to come. I stood there, stunned, in disbelieving of this wicked turn out. I didn't even notice my lawyer Michael waving his hands in my direction to get my attention. It finally took a couple of claps in the face for me to snap out of it.

I couldn't help but shake my head in shame, apologize and repeat,

"I'm done, Mike! I'm done!"

"Not just quite yet! I got some good news and some bad news," Michael said with a light grin on his face.

"Well... lay it on me. The *bad* news first." I slowly wiped the water from my eyes. Secretly I was hoping the bad news was really good news in disguise.

"Well the state was really trying to slam you and give you the max amount of time possible. But I was able to talk them out of that just now while on break. Erick, they are willing to offer you a couple of years because this is your first offense. With that being said, in Smithville, you are only required to serve 50% of your time. With good behavior you will be out in less than 10-11 months."

Michael attempted to go on as if jail time, period, was acceptable but I had to interrupt him.

"Listen, all I need to know is will this go on my record? Will it harm me in the future or will I be able to get a job once this is all said and done. Or what?"

"Well... yes," he said. "In fact, in a couple months or so I can help you get this expunged from your record. And as a suggestion, you may still be eligible to join the military."

The statement was made a joke which in light of the situation, didn't sound like a bad idea at all.

The judge entered the room shortly after with a thick stack of papers in hand. I assumed one of them contained the verdict.

While rambling through the papers he looked my direction with eye contact that only made me sweat. I felt like he silently let me know that I was in for a long haul.

"Please stand, Mr. Erick Martinez!"

"Yes, sir," I replied as I stood tall with my hands behind my back and my knees trembling.

He then announced that the papers in his hands were in fact the verdict and that no matter what the papers stated that this was not the end of the world.

"Yes sir," I agreed. Prayers started cycling through my thoughts as I clinched my hands together in anticipation. My palms were perspiring and my nerves were a wreck.

"According to the case provided, you were charged with many felonies, murder being the most serious of them all. This charge alone could send you to prison for more than 20 years." It was a dramatic pause then he continued. "With the evidence provided, the court has found you not guilty."

"Thank you, Jesus!" I sighed with relief as tears began to fall from my eyes heavily.

My wife also stood and clapped loudly, "Thank you, Jesus!" I could hear her repeat.

"Mr. Martinez, you were also charged with drug trafficking and attempt to deliver.

With the evidence provided, Mr. Martinez, the court has found you,"

the judge stopped dramatically for another second, "guilty.

"Now, because this was your first offense," he continued, "I'm sentencing you to 6 years and 10 months in jail. You will always need to pay a fine of $10,000."

As he finished reading the papers, Michael reached his hand

over to me. "We can still fight this. It's not over yet!"

I only held my head down. All I could do is turn to my wife to witness her burst out in tears.

"I love you, Erick!" she said through sobs. "We will get through this, baby!" She shouted as she shoved her way past officers who tried to keep her on the pew side of the courtroom. She gave me a brief hug only to be interrupted and separated from the guards. They threatened to put her into custody should she not behave. So I informed her to relax and listen.

I already felt like I had hurt her enough and regretted everything about this trial. I do not know what I would do if she was held in contempt because of me. I wanted her to be happy, but most of all, free.

But that was a long time coming. Separate officers in the court room started to walk my way. They soon placed hand cuffs on me and carried me away to begin my long, lengthy sentence.

Chapter 3

I sat up on my top bunk and placed my two hands up to my face to say a quick prayer thanking God for the position he put me in. I had a lot of time to realize that within a couple weeks I would be a free man.

Even after spending many years incarcerated, for doing crimes I did not commit, I could honestly say, that praying was a safe haven and totally changed my outlook on my situation. Through God's vision, time to think clearly, and thoroughly, I was able to come up with a business plan for as soon as I touched the road outside of here.

"Lunch time!" the guards yelled as all the cell doors on the block unlocked.

As they opened, inmates stepped out and proceeded in a line down to the cafeteria.

While walking and brainstorming more about business plans I felt a soft tap on my shoulder.

"What's good, boss? You should really watch where you're going." I guess I had dazed off in my thoughts. But he was allowing me to step in the line.

"Thanks, man…"

"My name Shawn Shawn but most people call me OG Shawn

Shawn. What you rap or is some type of business man? I see you over there constantly writing and coming up with stuff. If anything, I get out in a few weeks, I got a couple of big connects that can make anything happen."

"Hey, hurry up! The food is getting cold!" Someone yelled in the far back of the line. From the tone of his voice I could tell he was either irritated or woke up on the wrong side of the bed. Shawn Shawn did not budge, he simply continued about his connections out in the real world. We were almost next to grab our food trays and from the corner of my eyes I saw three guys come up behind us. One had a tattoo that read "Almighty Smith Gang". I knew that meant this situation was taking a turn south.

"Hey! You didn't hear me?" The tattooed guy shouted at us. "Hurry up! And stop gossiping like some little women!"

"Yeah! Get your food, I'm hungry." Another one of the guys said in a threatening tone.

Almost on cue, Shawn turned around with the quickness and began to swing, knocking out two of the guys instantly cracking their jaws and knocking out their teeth. I quickly grabbed the third by the collar as he tried to sneak an attack on Shawn. Once I got him, something came over me and I just proceeded to beat him to a bloody mess.

Other inmates watching simply stared in amazement, probably wondering how two quiet guys,

who keep to themselves, could be so aggressive and lethal. It felt as though minutes went by and I was still swinging and stomping. All of the built up anger I had pent up inside me from over the recent years was finally released as I had finally found something or should I say someone to take it out on. Guards pushed their way through the crowd breaking everyone up and Shawn and I were escorted from the lunch room before a major riot or brawl was initiated.

The correctional officers took us to an interrogation room.

"What is wrong with you guys?"

One of the guards questioned with a slight laugh.

I assume he thought the fight was funny.

"Do you know you could've really killed those guys out there? From what were was told,

one of the guys were knocked unconscious; the others suffered severe injuries to the face and ribs."

"Well that ought to teach them a lesson," Shawn replied a little smug.

I started to laugh at his comment as I finally began to cool down.

"We really did do a number on those guys, man."

We all chuckled.

We were released and escorted back to our dorms. Shawn informed me of his own plots and plans for when he was free again. I couldn't help but notice how similar his strategies were to mines. So I opened up about my plans as well and before

I knew it I had a really close friend.

We spent the rest of the day just reminiscing and bouncing ideas off of each other. We actually never realized how close our cells were until it was time for roll call.

Ever since I been in here I stayed away from fights, even arguing.

I just been quiet and stayed to myself, especially after seeing my roommate get murdered within months of being here. I also had not received a letter or visitation from my wife in about eleven months. I did not have anyone to vent or talk to, let alone let real emotions out around.

I was once on top of the world. I saw everything I worked hard for crumble in the blink of an eye. It felt great to have someone with the same ambitions I have in my presence.

As days went on, both me and Shawn's release date was coming close. I didn't notice how much of a great chef he was and he was teaching me some great meals he learned from a friend at an old job he had, even with the prison limited ingredients and cooking supplies.

"Hey, Erick! Try this dish! I'm calling it 'Smith Crispy Treats'!" Shawn yelled. I tried anything he made without any hesitation, and just like many times before I took one bite and fell instantly in love. Shortly after that he introduced me to another dish he called 'The Smith Syrup Sandwich' which to me was just as good.

While finishing the last bite I suggested he should put all these recipes in a cook book or possibly open up a restaurant.

"Hey, that doesn't sound too bad, Martinez," Shawn said while looking at me as if he had came up with an even greater idea on

top of that. "Why don't you run it with me?"

Chapter 4

After three and a half years in prison I was finally being released.

The one thing that weighed heavily on my mind was why my wife stopped coming to visit and did not keep in touch. It was not like her at all.

I decided to call up my cousin, Calvin Jackson. I knew he lived nearby, he had a car and would be willing to take me to my house. And he did.

We pulled up to my house and this weird, uncomfortable feeling came over me. Something was not right but I tried to ignore it as I walked to the door and rang the bell with a bright smile across my face. I was hoping that she would answer the door and greet me with a huge hug. I missed her hugs, her hands, her smile, her voice—*her*. But as the door knob turned, to my surprise, it was my lawyer Michael in a bath robe standing before me.

"Hey?" He was startled. "What's up, sir? How have you been? Didn't expect to see you here so soon—" I quickly interrupted him.

"Where in the hell is my wife? Why are you here?" I felt a storm of anger brewing as the more questions and thoughts cycled through my mind.

"Oh, her?" Mike responded in a sarcastic tone.

I couldn't help but shove him down to the ground as I raged in the house looking through every room yelling my wife's name. She stood in the laundry room near a pile of clothes she was folding in shock and disbelief like a thief caught red-handed. I tapped loudly three times on the washing machine to break her short spell.

"Oh, hey umm... Erick! How are you? Didn't expect you here anytime soon." She try to play it down but couldn't find her words. Sensing my irritation and rage she attempted to go on about how she tried to tell me that she had moved on and when she decided to move on it was with my lawyer.

"How could you do that though?" I yelled. "After all these years you just gone throw it away just like that? What have I done to you?" I screamed at the top of my lungs. "You stopped visiting. You stopped writing. You didn't even accept any of my calls. You could have at least told me face to face the last time you saw me."

"I'm sorry, Erick! I'm *so* sorry,"

she started crying, reaching out for a hug. Thinking I was going to reach back out and accept her apology I then shoved her arms away, turned around and stormed out the house. She followed behind me a few paces repeatedly shouting out to me how sorry she was and wanted to work things out. I ignored her pleas as I returned to my cousin's car and drove off. Just half way down the street I asked Calvin to pull over. He asked what exactly happened in the house.

"You okay?" Calvin asked. "All I saw was buddy fall to the floor and you storm in and out the house."

"Man, it's my wife. She stopped replying to my letters and phone calls. She even stopped coming to visit me while I was locked up."

"Man, you already know what you got to do though. Just file a divorce and execute the plans you said you had plotted all while you was locked up."

"You know what, you're right. I know it's a lot going on with me right now but do you mind if I spend a couple nights at your place? Just until the ball is rolling and I promise you I will give you back every dime I owe you."

Calvin agreed to me staying and I could not thank him enough.

He instantly interrupted me stating that we are blood cousins and that he wouldn't accept a dime from me.

As we finally made it to his house I couldn't help but break down and cry.

"Why me," I asked God. "Why me?"

"You good, big Cuz?" Calvin looked at me strangely but my issues were all over face really. "Look, we are blood cousins. It is in our blood to fall and get right back up way harder then we were in the first place. Just look at all the people in our family who have done it already." It was true.

I took his words into consideration as time went on. It

seemed like the more I prayed, night in and night out, it formed everything into place as I planned. In just a few short weeks the ideas me and Shawn Shawn came up with together were coming to life. The grand opening of our new restaurant, Smith Delights, was just right around the corner.

"Aye Calvin?" I asked with a confident look on my face while walking into his job, "would you like to be a manager at the new restaurant that we are opening up?"

"Yeah, no doubt!" He said as he threw down his goggles and apron. He walked towards me giving me the tightest hug ever. "Thanks big Cuz, I knew you could do it!"

"No man! I couldn't have done it without you though, thanks for believing in me."

"Man! Enough with all this mushy stuff let's go get this bag," he said with a bright smile on his face. As we walked out together I couldn't help but think that he just quit his job.

"So you just gone walk out like that?"

"Yeah man, why not? I *am* a manager at you and Shawn's restaurant.

What would I need with them anyways?" I looked at him and

busted out laughing. *Ring ring ring*! I reached in my pocket to see who it was calling me and to my surprise it was Shawn. "Hey! What's up, fool?! We was just talking about you!"

"Man forget all that!" he said, "How about we were asked by the mayor to up the date to our grand opening due to high demands?"

"Wait, what are you talking about?" I stood there in a stuck position. "What do you mean?" I could tell Shawn was grinning as he explained that the word somehow got out about our business and was spreading like wild fire around the neighborhood.

"That's why we were asked to move that grand opening day for our restaurant to tomorrow morning, bro."

"Wow,"

I said excitedly. Absolutely everything I prayed for was shaping up into exist just as fast.

I hung up with Shawn and begin to tell Calvin the great news. He too couldn't help but feel the over whelming joy as he then shouted out "Yessss!"

We hugged each other and started heading back home to get ready for the big premiere opening the following morning.

Waking up in the morning while getting dressed I couldn't help but thank God for so much and preparing me for this day. It was kind of like I predicted my future. Calvin and I got in the car and started to head towards the restaurant.

I couldn't help but notice the long line wrapped around the corner.

"Yo! Over here!" Shawn yelled at the top of his lungs to get our attention. He directed us to park and come in through the back door as the front door was flooded with people.

Right before it was time to announce the opening Shawn,

Calvin and I walked through the front door allowing everyone to crowd around and cheer. We took pictures and shook more hands we could count. When everything was said and done we stood in front of the big red ribbon and were handed the life size scissors to cut it together.

The customers flooded in one by one as me, Shawn and Calvin stood outside for a brief moment in amazement before getting to work. A new chapter was opening up for each of us and I was so grateful to God for allowing me to be a part of it.

I realized that even through all my trials and tribulations, I can honestly say, that prayers do change things!

Amen

The end